The Secret Night World of Cats

Helen Landalf
Illustrated by Mark Rimland

A SMITH AND KRAUS BOOK FOR KIDS

The Secret Night World of Cats

For information regarding permission, write to:
Smith and Kraus, Inc.
PO Box 127, Lyme, NH 03768

A Smith and Kraus Book for Kids
Published by Smith and Kraus, Inc.

Library of Congress Cataloging-in-Publishing Data
Landalf, Helen.
The secret night world of cats / by Helen Landalf.
p. cm.
Summary: Amanda climbs out her bedroom window to find her cat Tabby and enters a magical place
where kittens dance beneath the moon and flying cats sail from tree to tree like bats.
ISBN·1-57525-117-5
[1. Cats—Fiction. 2. Night—Fiction. 3. Lost and found possessions—Fiction.] I. Title.
PZ7.L231655Sg 1997
[E]—dc21   97-29775
CIP
AC

Manufactured in the United States of America
Design and Layout by Kathleen Blavatt

First Edition: June 1998
10 9 8 7 6 5 4 3 2 1

Dedication

*This book is dedicated to my cat Raku
for many years of faithful friendship.*

Acknowledgements

*Thank you to Kathleen Blavatt
for her patience and dedication in working
with Mark Rimland on the illustrations.*

*Thank you to Pamela Gerke and Daniel Johnson
for their feedback and advice on the text.*

*Thank you to Marisa Smith and Eric Kraus
for their help and support in creating this book.*

Tabby was Amanda's best friend.
They played together every day, and
each night Tabby slept contentedly in
her little basket beside Amanda's bed.

But one moonlit night
Amanda awakened to find
Tabby's basket empty! So
out the bedroom window she
climbed in search of her missing cat.

In the cool evening garden behind her house Amanda saw a white Persian cat batting at a tiny silver fish in the pond…

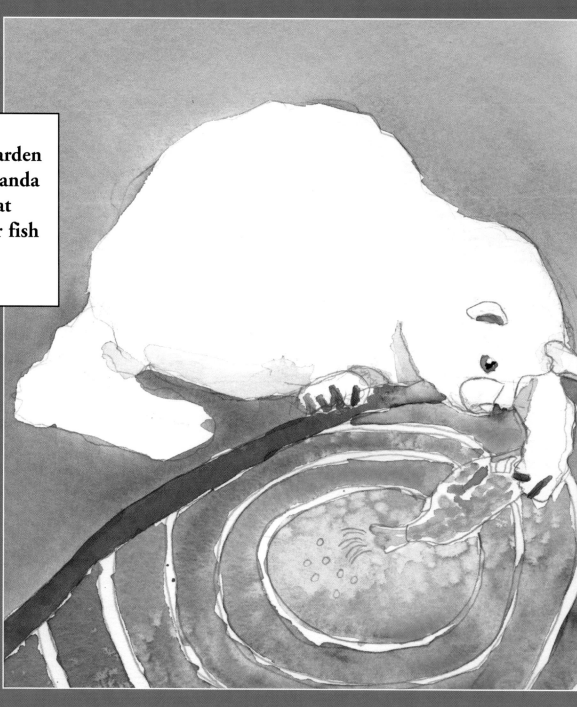

...a sleek Siamese cat stalking a jewel-winged butterfly...

...and two calico cats leaping into the air chasing moonbeams.

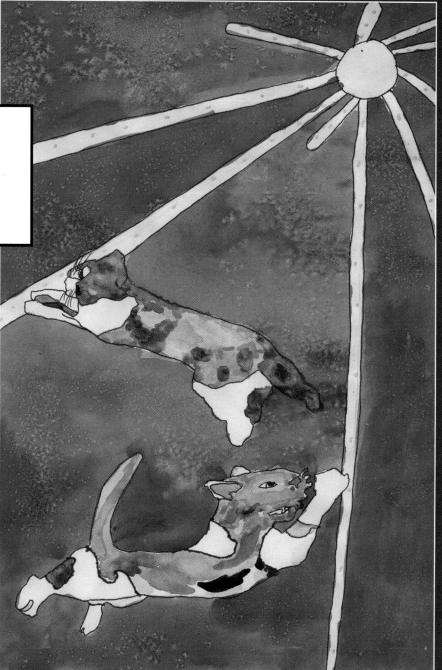

But Tabby was
nowhere to be seen.
Anxiously, Amanda
ventured deeper
into the night world
to search for her.

Slipping through the garden gate, Amanda entered a dark alley where three lean, hungry alley cats yowled angrily at her from atop a broken fence.

Suddenly they began to fight and hiss over a scrap of old fish beside a garbage can.

"I hope they haven't hurt my Tabby!" Amanda thought fearfully. More worried than ever, she began to run swiftly through the streets of the sleeping city and out into the open fields beyond.

"Here, kitty kitty," she called hopefully.

But in the starlit meadow she caught sight only of a tiny golden kitten sniffing a buttercup…

...a fluffy orange cat listening to the sad songs of night birds...

...and two young black and white cats tumbling in the silver grass.

So she ran on through the fields, over a hill and into the dark forest surrounding the city.

Amanda began to move more cautiously, for she knew that the forest was full of magic. Under every curling fern lay a tiny kitten purring and kneading the spongy green moss.

An elegant Abyssinian sat proudly on a rock, surrounded by thousands of flickering fireflies.

Suddenly, in the thick silence of the night Amanda caught a glimpse of Tabby running by! Following her into a clearing, Amanda came upon a wondrous sight: hundreds of cats dancing in a circle beneath the moon, swaying and weaving gracefully under the stars.

Tabby grabbed Amanda's hand, and she found herself whirling, spinning and cavorting in the midst of the dancers.

Amanda danced joyfully, happy to have found her pet. Then she looked more closely at the cat next to her.

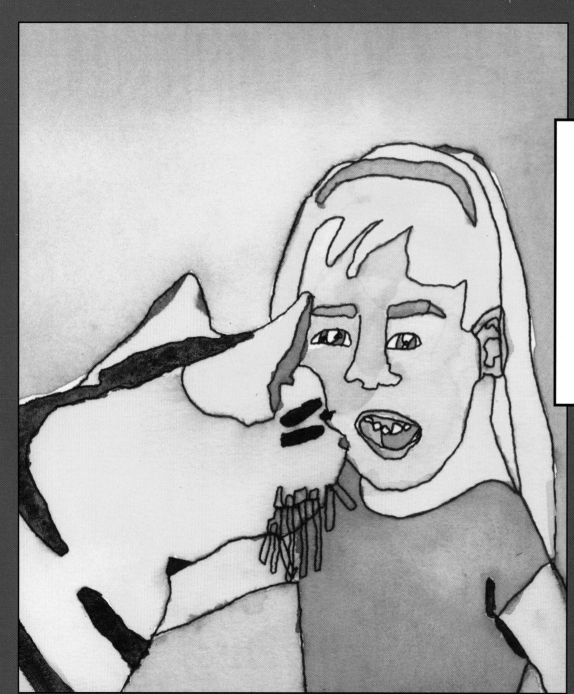

"You aren't my Tabby!" she cried as she pulled away from the strange cat's grasp. "Oh, do stay," implored the cat in a rich, mewing voice. But Amanda was already gone, desperate to find her lost friend.

Amanda ran breathlessly deeper and deeper into the forest until she reached the silent world where giant jungle cats stalk.

"Perhaps Tabby has gone to visit her relatives," she murmured timidly to herself. In the trees just ahead was a lioness resting her giant chin on huge paws, watching the moon through half-closed eyes.

Nearby, her cubs purred loudly as they lapped from a milky stream.

In the shadows a
tiger's stripes shivered
in the night breeze.

Woosh!
Amanda ducked
just in time to avoid
being hit by a
flying cat!
Hundreds of them
sailed from tree
to tree like bats.

Then, without warning, the forest became silent. In the silence Amanda felt twelve pairs of yellow eyes glowing at her from behind a thicket. Closer and closer the eyes came, staring at Amanda without blinking.

"Who are you?" whispered Amanda. "Why are you looking at me?"

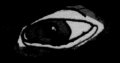

But the eyes just kept staring, coming nearer and nearer. Amanda was so frightened that she didn't know what to do...so she began to sing! She sang loud and strong and true. Her voice echoed across the hush of the jungle. As she sang the eyes grew smaller and smaller, disappearing into the darkness.

Amanda felt a soft furry head rub against her leg. She looked down in joyful disbelief.

"Tabby!" she laughed. "Where in the world have you been?"

Tabby just swished her tail as if to say "follow me."

Amanda followed Tabby to the deepest, thickest part of the jungle. Hidden among the creepers and vines was a dark cave. Amanda followed Tabby inside.

"Mew. Mew. Mew."
Inside the cave was a
tiny kitten crying in
sadness as it searched
for its lost mother.
Amanda watched as
Tabby picked up the
kitten by the scruff of
the neck. She followed
as Tabby carried the
kitten through the
jungle to a hollow tree
stump. Inside the tree
stump a mother cat
lay sadly, fearing she
would never see her
kitten again. Tabby
gently dropped the
kitten into the stump
beside its mother.

The mother cat's eyes lighted up with joy. She licked her baby, purring loudly.

"Thank you," she said to Tabby in the secret language of cats. Then the kitten and its mother curled up together and slept.

Amanda proudly scooped Tabby into
her arms and carried her gently back
into the jungle, through the forest,
across the fields, through the narrow
alleys and streets of the sleeping city,
into the garden and through the
bedroom window. Amanda and Tabby
slept in each other's arms till dawn, each
dreaming of her own special adventure
in the secret night world of cats.

The End

HELEN LANDALF

Helen Landalf is author of *Moving is Relating: Teaching Interpersonal Skills Through Movement in Grades 3-6, Moving the Earth: Teaching Earth Science Through Movement in Grades 3-6,* and co-author of *Movement Stories for Young Children* with Pamela Gerke, all published by Smith & Kraus, Inc. Helen makes her living as a dance educator and has been teaching, choreographing and performing dance in the Seattle area since 1987, with an emphasis on teaching creative and modern dance to children. She is on the faculty of the Creative Dance Center in Seattle and has served as an Artist in Residence for the Montana Public Schools. She frequently presents workshops for preschool and classroom teachers on integrating dance into the basic curriculum. Helen currently resides in Seattle, Washington with her cat Raku.

MARK RIMLAND

Mark Rimland, the brother of author Helen Landalf, was born with autism in San Diego in 1956. He grew up in a time when relatively little was known about this perplexing syndrome. In response to his son's disability, Dr. Bernard Rimland established the Autism Research Institute.

Mark is a savant artist. He studies art privately with Kathleen Blavatt, and in classes at a center for developmentally disabled adults. Mark's whimsy, contour line style and love for animals is apparent in his artwork. He is gaining a national reputation for both his traditional and computer-generated artwork.

He has appeared on PBS *People in Motion, Breaking the Silence Barrier, Computer Chronicals,* CBS *This Morning* show, CNN, NTV *Art Time* in Japan. His artwork has been displayed in numerous galleries, shows and publications. Many of Mark's pieces have been reproduced in greeting cards and prints for the Autism Research Institute, Special Olympics, St. Madeleine Sophie's Center, and others. For information about Mark Rimland and his artwork, write: Autism Research Institute, Adams Ave., San Diego, CA 92116